# FLASHES OF VICE

## Volume I

*a collection of flash fiction stories*

# VINCENT DE PAUL

First published online (Print-on-Demand) on CreateSpace in 2013
Kindle Edition by Mystery Books, an Imprint of Mystery Publishers – 2013
Smashwords Edition by Mystery Books – 2017

A CIP record of this book is available from the Kenya National Library
US Library of Congress Catalogue Number 2019350230

This Paperback Edition

ISBN: 978-9914-9953-7-4

Published by:
Mystery Publishers (K) Ltd,
P.O. BOX 18016–20100
Nakuru, Kenya.
www.mysterypublisherslimited.com
Email: info@mysterypublisherslimited.com
Tel: +254 718 429 184

Typeset in Palatino Linotype pt.12 by Mystery Publishers
First printing: Kenya, 2016
Reprint: 2017, 2018, 2019, 2020
Revisions: 2014, 2015, 2016, 2017, 2022


Printed and bound in Kenya.

Acclaim for *Flashes of Vice: Vol I*

Using flash fiction, a style of fictional literature of extreme brevity ... Vincent has bequeathed his readers with *Flashes of Vice,* a collection of tell-them-as-they-happen-in-real-life stories.

*The Sunday Nation,*
*26 January 2014*

It makes a good read.

*Principal Education Secretary*
*Kenya National Examinations Council*

Short and crisp as usual: brief but nice ...

*NaijaStories*

... it's an impressive book ... The brevity of the stories is also commendable. Some stories are so short and great that one can complete reading them in under one minute.

*Lighten Up*
*(www.nancyoyula.wordpress.com)*

# Other Books by Vincent de Paul

## Flash Fiction

*Flashes of Vice: Vol III (2017)*
*Flashes of Vice: Vol II (2014)*

## Novels

*Twisted Times: The Phantom (2020)*
*Inevitable Desires: First Love (2019)*
*Twisted Times: Son of Man (2015)*

## Poetry

*First Words (2011)*
*Holy Emotions (2012)*
*Flights of Poetic Fancy (2014)*
*Holy Crimes (2014)*

## Non-Fiction

*The Fundamentals of Strategic Writing (2022)*

## Anthologies

*Our Stories Redefined Anthology by Mystery Publishers (2022)*
*Our Stories Redefined Anthology by Mystery Publishers (2021)*
*When a Stranger Called by 13 Kenyan Authors (2020)*
*Through the Journey of Hope by Writers Guild Kenya (2016)*
*Black Communion: Poems of the New Age African Poets (2013)*

*"To run away from trouble is a form of cowardice..."*

**Aristotle**

# Contents

# FLASHES OF VICE

Lorem ipsum

# Crime & Justice

# Daddy's Girl

*Friday 13<sup>th</sup>, 3:45 p.m.;*
*Central Police Station,*
*Nairobi, Kenya.*

"STUPID POLICEMAN," LOYCE OYUGA SCREAMED. "You don't know whom you are playing with."

"*We msichana mang'aa, nani alisema tuna-cheza hapa?*" the policeman said.

"My father is the Chief of Defence Forces, and the Minister for Internal Security is my uncle. You will kiss your pathetic career in the police force goodbye, and to cap it all, you'll go to jail."

"Shut up!" Inspector Lina Mulusi snapped, silencing Loyce and startling the Anti-Narcotics Unit detectives who had brought Loyce in.

Loyce had been arrested at the Jomo Kenyatta International Airport (JKIA) for being in possession of Class A heroin.

"All evidence is pinned to you. It is your bulimic belly that is securely carrying a truckload of the drugs, your designer clothes that were concealing your junk, Miss Mule," Inspector Lina said. "Not your dad's, junkie. And if the grapevine is anything to go by, your father is retiring tomorrow. If I were you, I'd try to persuade Dad to chunk off part of his send-off package to get me the best criminal lawyers around. The judges might decide to get you a few years or a hefty fine, or both, which of course, Dad will pay, or you will rot in jail, and no one will appeal."

"How very gracious of you," Loyce exclaimed. "You won't be in that tattered uniform by tomorrow, bitch."

Inspector Lina tried not to lose her cool.

Just then, Lina's phone rang. It was a strange number, but she picked up the call anyways.

"Inspector," the voice was more authoritative and stern than she expected. No one would have mistaken the Police Commissioner's voice, but she chose to play hard. After all, it was her phone.

"Yes, who's this?"

"I understand you have a suspected mule in custody."

"That's restricted information I can't divulge to third parties, especially to strangers," Inspector Lina said. "And I have work to do, not to talk to intimidating strangers …"

"Of course not. This is the Police Commissioner."

"Yessir."

"That's the daughter of the Chief of Defence Forces you have there. I understand she was arrested in connection with drugs?"

"Yes, sir. She's been charged. She is appearing in court on Monday. She is staying in our custody over the weekend."

"Good, Inspector. Your work is commendable."

"You are endorsing my decision to detain her?"

"Absolutely. Otherwise, you wouldn't be

doing your work effectively if I interfered."

"Yessir," Inspector Lina said. "And sir, may I ask you how you came by this info to call me?"

"Inspector, it's not in your pay grade to ask me how I come about my intel, and I am the Police Commissioner, but I'll tell you anyway. I just got off the phone with the Minister for Internal Security. He's your suspect's uncle. He says he's had enough of his niece. His brother, the CDF, runs to him whenever his daughter is in trouble. Turns out she's the drug baron we've been hunting. She's also a user and has drained the family for long. They now want her to get what's coming to her.

"However, that's not why I gave you the go-ahead. We won't be doing our work if we let ourselves be controlled by the powers that be. *Utumishi Kwa Wote*. Sounds familiar?"

"Yes, sir," Inspector Lina said, her palpitating heart almost jumping into her throat. "Sorry for my earlier crude ..."

"Inspector, I did not promote you to be tossed around by every *body*, and anybody."

"Yes, sir."

The Police Commissioner hung up, but one

question hung in the air, 'How did the top cop get her number?'

Inspector Lina stared at the mule with disdain. Loyce's face was a thousand shades of spite, arrogance, goad, malice, and intimidation.

"We're done here, Loyce," she said. "You appear in court on Monday morning. Detectives, take the suspect to the cells and hand her over to Selina, the custody sergeant."

Now, all the walls tumbled down, and Loyce's face turned from pale to a thick hue of blue. Just then, the reality of what was about to happen hit her, and her eyes pleaded guilty and cried meekness coupled with penitence, and would she be released? She would pay anything. God, going to those cells was an imagination she couldn't allow.

"Please, I'll do anything—anything—for you, but don't take me there," Loyce protested.

Inspector Lina just shrugged.

"Sorry, there's nothing I can do."

"Please, I'll give you anything. I've got money. I'll give you anything. Just name your price."

"That won't help. You've just added attempting to bribe a police officer to your charges," said Inspector Lina.

Loyce's eyes flashed as though they had been struck by lightning in the cloudy sky of her mind. "Please, don't do this to me. I can pay you. I will pay you. I promise."

"No deal," the inspector said. "At least I won't be naked come tomorrow; my tattered uniform will be intact."

# Darkest Place of All

I WATCHED THE CASKET OF my once oh-so beloved beautiful wife being lowered electrically into the grave.

Charlene and Shirley, our two beautiful daughters, 13 and 15 years old, let out one last deafening scream. They almost jumped into the marble-tiled grave after their mother.

Of all people, Charlene and Shirley had been the most affected by the cold, bloody murder of their mother, my lovely wife of 15 years. What a tragic loss?

Her father, a wealthy businessman and a veteran politician, had vowed to do whatever it took to bring to book her killer. He ought to. No one has the right to take anyone's life.

As I tried to hold back Charlene and Shirley, I couldn't help thinking of Mandy. She had been such a darling to the world. In death, she was like a miserable-people magnet.

But now it was over.

Only that she had taken to the grave a very big secret—her killer's identity.

Both Mandy and I knew that her murderer would never be caught. Her murder would go down in the books of unsolved murders history.

The murderer had done all it took to ensure that even the much-famed American CSI couldn't get him and had allowed her to see his face before she died; she was going to die after all.

I know all this because I killed Mandy, my sweet wife.

Fifteen years of deception is a long time. From the first day we met, Mandy had been a whore all along, an escort for the stinking rich scum of this republic, and I fell for her head over heels. *A Campus Diva for the Rich*, that's what she was for 15 years.

Even after graduation from the University

of Nairobi and our marriage, she continued peddling her cunt for whatever God knew. I loved her, gave her everything, yet she lied to me and called me babe.

How could she?

Well, the truth was the bitterest pill I was forced to swallow when I discovered it.

How could she? I loved her.

Fine, the truth is the darkest place of all.

# Guilty as Charged

IN PRISON TWENTY YEARS, I got out today. No one would have said it was a sentence too lenient or an amnesty too early.

My mama always said a mother would kill for her kids. *Should* kill for her kids.

One chilly morning, just as I was getting home from work, my anorexic, pathologically thin, model-beautiful preteen daughter rushed to me naked, crying.

What she had been telling me all along and what I had been ignoring—because I trusted too much, leaving no room for doubt—came hurtling back. My self-proclaimed pathological liar-cum-womaniser-morphed-sexual-predator husband had raped her—for the umpteenth time.

I checked my daughter's insides; she was wet.

My beloved, wretched husband of thirteen years, whom I too had neglected due to my job demands, emerged from our daughter's room in a post-coital trance, not even caring to spare me the sight of his rumpled pyjamas. What father preys on his daughter despite how immodest she appears?

All my sensei-inculcated tactics and many police-paid-hours in a Japanese dojo came instinctively. A round-house pirouette got him by surprise. Before he hit the ground, I had already put two bullets in his heart with my service revolver.

It was a high-profile case with a high-octane media frenzy. I was now part of statistics of rising cases of police officers killing their spouses. The only twist was that I did not end my life in the process of giving crime reporters a field day.

'Guilty as Charged' was my plea.

For 20 years, I have lived with hard, die-hard incorrigible criminals caged like animals at Lang'ata Women's Maximum Security Prison, people I had sworn to hunt.

That love for my Sweet Tracy has kept me alive in prison, but now I am out.

I would be glad to go back there if someone ever laid a finger on my daughter.

# Hit List

IT IS MUCH EASIER FOR a two-hump camel to go through the eye of a needle than for a poor man to enter the kingdom of lucre and subscribe to the trillionaires' club. Blessed are the poor, for they shall inherit the kingdom of heaven.

It started with the Inspector General of police. It was his *mbois* in blue who started the crackdown on us. He ordered them and gave the green light for *Operation Nasa Mianda-rati*. Well, biz is down, and every town in the country is too hot for our operatives—thanks to the top cop. In his police-reformed mind, he refused a too-good-to-turn-down offer.

Our bosses' names have been making headlines: too bad and unheard of in this business. Despite stashing the briefcase that the IG turned down, plus a bonus, the Minister for Internal Security still tabled the names of our bosses in parliament. What a shocker it was! He double-crossed us. Too bad for him. The whole world, America and Britain leading, have come down on our bosses like a ton of a thousand bricks. That's why that terrible accident had to happen. Our condolences to the friends and family of the minister; there wouldn't have been any other way.

Others, our next kingpins, they dragged to court. In her justice-must-be-served convoluted mind, the Lady Justice took the money yet convicted them. Here's the deal she offered: she would convict them but release them after the appeal—please the public and at the same time keep the part of her bargain. That's not how it works. Even the Mafia knows this. Fine, people are mourning. I feel for the bereaved, but surely, why be so avaricious?

That was the beginning. We had to go for the scum first. Now we are going for the trash.

We know the police resell what they seize from us through a network of street dealers. Imagine that! They are getting rich from our expense, reaping where they did not sow.

We know each and every one of them.

From Inspector to Constable.

Watch out!

# Kidnapped

*Nairobi, Kenya;*

SOPHIE LEFT THE CARNIVORE AT 6:30 p.m. and decided to walk home, a fifteen-minute walk.

Everywhere, and in all directions, people walked and talked—life a beehive of human activity—going about their lives like nothing was going on.

Glancing around to ensure she was safe, she realised there was still enough light to qualify as daytime. Despite the security measures she had been told to observe—to be more aware of her surroundings, not to be Facebooking, tweeting, or listening to music while walking—she fell victim to her foible and plugged her iPod earphone buds into her ears and also gave in to the temptation of Facebooking as she ambled home.

She walked on, Rihanna's *Russian Roulette* playing on her ears while chatting on FB, liking what her friends posted and sharing their pictures as she commented on their statuses after writing gibberish electronic graffiti on their Facebook walls.

Sophie was completely unaware of the two men following her. She took a narrow street, a shortcut, and found herself walking alone. She looked over her shoulder and saw the two men, but she was closer to her destination—home.

She didn't feel concerned at first, not until she glanced over her right shoulder and saw the men running, catching up on her, closing in. Within no time, they were onto her. One of the men slammed her to a wall, and before she could scream, an adhesive tape was stuck to her lips, sealing them as though to keep a secret. Plastic cables lashed her wrists and legs together.

A sharp prick on her neck, as that of a

hypodermic, brought a thick drapery of darkness that festooned her vision.

Sophie came to four hours later. She was lying on a bed, her arms tied and anchored behind her head. Her legs, too, were roped to the bed's metal frame. And then she made another discovery—she was naked, a white sheet draped between her legs.

A new kind of fear swept through her like cold fire, and she almost passed out. She couldn't be sure, but it felt like she had been over-raped.

She surveyed the room—it was odd, everything seemingly rustic. That was it; she was somewhere no one would find her. The only way was to talk her way out of this nightmare, survive, live, and fight another day. As all this went through her mind, she realised she was not alone.

"Hello, beautiful," a hoarse male voice said. "Ain't it kinda wonderfully romantic?"

That's when realisation tumbled onto her like a ton of a thousand bricks.

She knew that voice, knew it very well.

It was her disgruntled lover. He had been stalking her, threatening her if she didn't give in to his advances (in his wildest wet dreams), driving her crazy.

Well, she'd play by his rules if she wanted to get out of this nightmare, she decided. Sleep with the much-loathed enemy; even sell part of her soul to the devil.

"See, Willy, I could do what you want. You know you don't have to do this," Sophie said. "Sorry I have been a bitch, playing hard to get. It was just a game."

But she had a plan. Once she had the opportunity, she'd kick him in the balls, where it hurt most. She knew enough judo to disable him, as big as he was. Then she'd run like hell for her life.

"You don't seem to understand, do you?" Willy said. "This is a game, too."

With that, Willy tore away the sheet between her legs and forced himself inside her for the umpteenth time. He raped her for hours until she could take no more, then climbed off her.

"Yes, you could do what I want, but would you do it?" Willy asked her. "The game has just started. It's you whom I want. Let's call Daddy; perhaps he'll make us rich."

"Please," Sophie pleaded. "My father will

give you whatever you want. Just let me go."

"That's the spirit, dear," Willy snorted. "Dad's gonna pay your dowry, then we'll elope."

# Killer No.13

'ONE SHOT, ONE KILL.' SNIPER motto. That's what they taught us anyway. That was once upon a time. A life long gone. Another lifetime.

It was at the Kenya Army School of Infantry. The training was vigorous and dangerous.

First, I trained as a Recon Ranger, then a Special Forces sniper. I was Killer No.13. Lucky 13, enhe! Turned into a razor-sharp weapon, a killing machine.

Then I was enrolled for a secret hit squad that never existed, and it doesn't exist. Our missions were TOP SECRET. We eliminated the highest value targets that could threaten national and regional, make that international, security.

The only problem was that the pay was paltry. You know what the government, especially the forces, is mean.

Solution? I went freelance. In the mansions of powers that be, I am respected, honoured, and a solution to all political and religious problems.

# Most Wanted



"HOW MUCH DOES A JUDGE cost?" my father asked me.

"That depends," I said.

"Well, that's all justice is about in this republic."

"What are you not telling me, Dad?"

He sighed deeply and said, "We lost the case, John. We lost."

"What? What do you mean? No way!"

"Yes. Apparently, there's no sufficient evidence."

I was about to sob. "Everybody knew it. Everybody knows it. It was our land. It is our land." I almost shouted at Dad. "And we all know that it was him who killed Grandpa. Why, Dad? Why?"

My father was his usual cool. "John, son, I hate to tell you this, but it's the truth. Life ain't fair; get used to it."

I felt like I could kill somebody. Hell, I could, and would, kill somebody.

"Thank God you're alive, John," my father told me after a while. "World of Richie Riches, they get their own breaks, and everyone else's too."

"Yeah, I get it. The rich just get richer, and the poor—"

"Whine like you."

That was 10 years ago.

And this is now.

I have a bounty of over a billion shillings on my head. I rob, with violence, and kill the rich—government officials, media moguls, academicians, church leaders, bankers, police, judges, military gooks and all.

I am the MOST WANTED man locally and internationally.

That's the bad thing.

The good thing is that I do it for the common man.

And I never gonna be caught.
Trust me on that!

# Officer Down

*Wednesday, 11:30 p.m.,*
*Nakuru, Kenya.*

SUPERINTENDENT RICHARD NIXON KIMANZI, A veteran police officer, honked the horn of his self-drive official police car for the gateman to open the gates for him at his Section 58 residence.

His house was a short distance from Nakuru town, a few metres from the railway line. There had been a lot of work at the office, paperwork to close his three-year-old case. The case had turned out to be expensive for the station, for it was not forthcoming. The only option was to close it and stack the file in the cabinet of unsolved cold cases. That's why he was getting home late after missing the family dinner for the third time.

Hardly had he entered his bedroom when his cell phone vibrated. The caller ID indicated 'Private', and apprehension of such calls gripped him. He never picked up anonymous calls, but he found himself answering this.

"I know the drugs and Mungiki connection to the spate of murders and robberies you want to solve," the caller said. "Meet me at Taidy's in thirty; I'll give you more info." And with that, the caller hung up.

The idea was alluring, but the thought of it was risky. However, Richard gave in to temptation and decided to take the risk. The caller had mentioned one fact that was known only to him and the government pathologist—the murder victims had traces of cocaine and heroin in their systems and a note, more like a calling card, forced down their throats or other orifices with Mungiki written on them. He had decided to hold on to this info so as not to cause alarm about the re-emergence and change of *modus operandi* of the outlawed sect.

The pressure mounting on him to close the case while every part of him wanted to catch the killer, or killers, brought ominous desperation. In fact, another murder had been reported at Lanet, near the 3rd Battalion the Kenya Rifles barracks.

He got the look he expected when he told his wife he'd be back by midnight. But he had to go.

On the way, he called units on patrol in the area to converge at the Club Taidy's. Whoever the caller was would sleep in the comfort of one of the cells at the Central Police station.

At the Kenyatta Avenue roundabout, he was flagged down by a traffic police officer— odd for traffic police to be on duty at this hour of the night in Nakuru. Seldom would you spot one after seven o'clock, 7:30 p.m. if you're that lucky.

"*Afande,* is there a problem?" the cop asked.

"Nay, just routine check," Richard answered. Well, that was true. Richard was known to prowl the streets at night, checking whether those on night patrols were actually doing their work and not up to some mischief.

"But you're supposed to be home. This is not your work. You should leave the streets to us."

"It doesn't cost a thing to lose a few hours' sleep to check on how you guys are doing," Richard told his junior officer. He liked the constable's confidence.

"Exactly," the policeman said. "That's why we want you to get a message to your colleagues, those whom you've rallied and think like you. You are interfering with us, and that must stop."

"It was you ..." realisation was like wavelets of a coming storm on a calm sea on Richard.

"Yes," the policeman replied, pulling the trigger of a concealed pistol.

The nine millimetre fired at point blank range. "You should have stayed where you belong. Get your fat pay slip and enjoy privileges that befit you; leave the streets we prowl to us. You were getting too close to us and made the connection that we are the most feared in Nakuru of late. If only you could get us better pay ..."

The traffic cop fired two more shots into

Richard's chest, then one headshot. He then turned and fired in the air, a kind of police-gangster shoot-out scene.

Street families that frequented Kenyatta Avenue outside Shik Park Hotel, Shoppers Paradise, and Tuskys Supermarket ran for cover, and prostitutes who had not yet been picked ducked into the nearby clubs that were almost closing—thanks to *Mututho Law*.

"Officer down! Officer down!" the traffic policeman yelled on his radio as he fired in the air.

# Ransom

WHEN I KIDNAPPED MYSELF AND sent a ransom demand to my scumbag father, I did not expect he'd pay.

But guess he did!

I am now happy in my new home away from home, a high-rise apartment building I bought with the ransom.

Occasionally, I tune in to home TV stations and see my picture on the screens: *'Melissa Young Aluoch, daughter of the media mogul and entrepreneur Wilson Aluoch, is still missing despite the 80 million shillings' ransom being paid …'* says the newscaster.

With an abusive father, in all senses of the

word, for 20 years, I walked out last month. No one would have guessed, even my oh-so-subservient mother, that the decision I had made was a decision too late. She never listened to me anyway.

Now, I am a citizen of another country. I am not gonna say which one for security reasons, with a new life and identity.

They call me Samantha Williams over here.

# Robbed by Flesh

TODAY'S YOUTH—OUR BELOVED SONS AND daughters—are worthless, good-for-nothing schmucks.

My beautiful wife, Lizzie, died seven years ago. The grief almost killed me, but I have at last accepted. Her only legacy to me is her undying love and the most precious gift on earth—our daughter, Joan. I treasure her so much, and I would do anything for her. Well, that's what I have done. She has everything in this whole wide, wild world.

Nonetheless, Jo is just like any other delinquent. Even after giving her the best education, and the most luxurious life, making her an epitome of envy by her peers, all she could do was rob me. I wish I could understand, but how could she?

When she was kidnapped three weeks ago, and her abductors demanded 10 million shillings' ransom, I did not hesitate. I could even give the whole world to secure her release.

However, even after paying the ransom, her abductors didn't keep their part of the bargain. That was until today in the morning when she came with tears in her eyes and confessed.

"It was Rob," she cried. "My boyfriend. We cooked everything up. Dad, I'm so sorry I stole from you." Like she was contrite.

How could she? She's the sole beneficiary of all my wealth.

I'm still wondering—why the hell did she come back?

# Stolen from the Grave

WHEN MY BILLIONAIRE MOTHER DIED, the responsibility of burying her fell on me, her love child, by default.

The obsequies were stunning and also touching. Mama Lucy Kibaki choir graced the occasion with heavenly melodies. As the requiem service ended, we all stood and sang my mother's favourite—*Nilianza Safari* by Rose Jeffa. Rose was there herself, now an old lady immortalised by her music, and she was honoured to perform her song for my mother, she said.

On the material day, the whole compound was a bazaar of automobiles. The gamut ranged from stretch limos for *waheshimiwas* to the latest Mercs and sports utilities for businessmen and celebrities. It was more of a celebration (of a life well lived) than a funeral.

Everyone who's anybody, or thought is, was there—cabinet ministers and their assistants, the vice president and the prime minister, famous actors and producers, real estate tycoons and investors, high and low—all to bid my mother thee farewell.

As I watched the casket being lowered to her final resting place, memories of another life, back when she was alive, and I was her only source of happiness—as she had told me on her death bed—all came back to me. I couldn't help but cry quarts.

Nonetheless, that was then, and this is now. Ghost family members have sprouted up from phantom family trees, including a dad who'd been MIA since sowing his wild oats in my mother, have come demanding their share of my mother's wealth even before the dust has settled off.

I stopped crying the minute the ground swallowed my mother up, leaving no trace of her save for her photos that constantly reminded me of her. The mourning period turned into a tussle over what my loving mother bequeathed me.

'Women don't own property' has been the mantra.

Even business partners, lawyers, and con-fidants—people my mother trusted most in her lifetime—are after a share of what she tirelessly worked for.

It's bad enough that society has become a bunch of amoral, money-grabbing nincom-poops. Worse still, it has turned into gangster wannabes, too.

# Sex & Sets

# Of Lovers and Cheaters

"I DID WHAT YOU WANTED," she said, staring at him. "I was angry at you for getting me pregnant, but I resented myself for letting it happen. I wished you to go away, but I guess I couldn't let go."

"Why do we have to go through this again, Rita?" he asked.

"Because we were both responsible and handled it badly."

"Rita, I am sorry about my reaction when I found out about everything. But that's behind us now, I hope."

"Yes, it is, but there is a problem," she took an exasperated sigh, wiped a thin film of sweat on her upper lip and continued. "I'm afraid I still love you. Hell, I love you."

"Rita, we talked about being friends. That's what I can offer."

"Yeah, I know that, especially after you have a romp in the sack for old times' sake."

"This shouldn't have happened, and we both know it."

"You are such a selfish bastard, as you always were. It hurt like hell when I terminated the pregnancy, knowing I had also lost you. 'Where do I go? What do I do?' I asked myself."

"You're a big girl, Rita; smart and intelligent. I am sure you will find a way."

"You don't seem to understand. It is LOVE, Steve. I've tried to move on, but I couldn't. You always come out of the blue and get to me."

"Please, I didn't want this."

"I may be that strong, miss independent, tough woman in public, but I am still a woman, a girl, deep inside, vulnerable and in need of love. To be precise, I am plain weak, weak for you, Steve."

"What makes you think I am any stronger?"

"I don't know," Rita replied plaintively.

"So, this is all this meeting was about, isn't it?"

"For Jove's sake, I am a woman, in case you haven't noticed, and I have needs."

"God, Rita. Cessy is a woman too, and Jackie, and in case you haven't realised, I'm surrounded by women. So, I know what the lot of you look like."

"Steve, I have tried to move on, a few guys, one-offs, and nightstands. None of those men has given me a sense of permanence. God, you made me feel like a woman, and that's what I want. I can see you in my room, in the tub, and smell you as I do my hair. Cripes, I love you, Steve."

"I've a family, Rita. A wife and a daughter I love very much."

"What's it that Cecilia has that I don't? Shapely legs, probably. Big tits, obvious. Tighter squeeze, I doubt. From what I know of her, which I doubt you know, I wonder what I lack. Plus, I have brains—which she doesn't."

Steve smirked. "That's my wife you are lambasting," he said, hackles beginning to rise. "And I love her so much. Will that do?"

"Yeah, and that's what you told me for three years."

"Look, I loved you, and I still do, differently. Cessy makes me feel safe; she's perfect for me."

"And you are perfect for me. You turned me into this fantasy girl I barely knew. I love that girl. That's what I want."

Her eyes were drooling. Wait a minute—do eyes drool? Well, Rita's did.

She saw the look on his face and knew what was coming next. "See Steve, how weak I am?"

He trembled, and a tingling waltzed in his loins. "Please, we can stop this when we both can."

"What now? For old times' sake, we've just had this truly ecstatic lovemaking I crave. Can't we have another round?"

"Nothing more happens. This never happened."

"But you just cheated on this Cessy wife woman you so much love." She saw a frisson cross his face. "Don't worry, I won't rat on you, but I want you, just a piece of you, on reasonable terms. I won't ask for more or demand you leave your Cessy. Heck, I'm too proud to play second fiddle. That won't suit me. But Steve, honest-to-God, I love you."

"What if I don't want to see you again? You know I am running for governorship this year."

"Your loss," Rita said. "And I guess Cessy knowing of this is not on your mind?"

"Cessy and I have no secrets," he told her.

"Then that's your problem. Go and empty your dirty little secret to her and the priest, but you just cheated on your wife."

"Don't you blackmail me, Rita."

"Not in the least, sweetie. If I were, you'd have already coughed a few millions by now," she said and gave him the wink.

She winked again, and that was all she needed to do. He pounced on her like a puma, climbed on top, and slid smoothly into her.

# Pregnancy

*Diary of a Rogue Hustler*

**21st May;**

I ENJOYED THE TORMENT OF suffering resignation I saw in their eyes, all of them. Men, when they have something to lose, are great investments.

John was a senatorial aspirant with a reputation to protect and a family to care about. When I presented him with the prospect of losing his political career and family, he coughed two million shillings to get me to procure an abortion (he still wants to keep coming to me on weekends and some nights). Well, I can't abort my baby, so he ended up buying me off with seven million shillings after so much haggling and signing a paper that granted him immunity against anything I might bring up in future. Fine with me. I will miscarry.

Jeff's a rich dad's kid. He's got a trust fund running into millions. The only problem is he's been using it without his dad's knowledge in collusion with his father's bank manager. When Dad hears about this, he'd practically kill him. So, when I told him I was pregnant for him, he almost went bonkers. Was I out of my mind? No. I was perfectly sane, and I wanted us to marry. But Jeff wants to make Daddy proud, and has the whole future ahead of him to live. He'd allow nothing to come in between. On humanitarian grounds, one million shillings for an abortion at the best hospital in the country was the deal.

Then there's Pastor Dane. I've been his secret lover since the senator introduced me to him and to his church and secured me a tender with his church. So there goes the fact that there's no man, or woman, of the cloth who does what they say. His case had both political and religious ramifications. His offertory returns, untaxed, run into tens of millions. I ended up with five million from him to establish myself as his secret family, then Ksh.500,000 monthly upkeep. I agreed to the terms and conditions, but he can keep the monthly upkeep. I ain't interested.

I've just got my new identification documents and removed the fake pregnancy but left the IUD intact.

Lying about being pregnant has given me some satisfaction, but what I enjoyed most was the shenanigans, the sampling of men and then lying there with eyes closed, pretending to enjoy it while planning everything in my mind and faking the big O.

Now, what I think of are the things the money would buy.

# Pregnant

"I'M PREGNANT," SHE BLURTED OUT.

She now had my attention.

"I'm pregnant, J …"

"I heard you," I said, a slight tinge of irritation getting the better of my voice.

A thousand things came to my mind, but what I said was what nearly all men say, "What are you going to do?"

"What are you going to do?"

"It's me who asked you."

"And I'm asking you. It's yours too."

"Are you sure …"

"What? You think I've been screwing behind your back?"

"No, I did not mean that."

"Then what? You're the only one I've been with. I was a virgin."

"Yeah, that I noticed. For God's sake, how the hell did you get pregnant? We were using protection always."

"Perhaps the condom burst and leaked or something."

"Well, that poses a problem."

There was a long silence, then she said, "We could marry. I'll be 18 next month."

Definitely, that's what I meant when I said it posed a problem.

A fast-forwarding movie of my dreams being ruined played in my mind—education, job, prosperity and a beautiful young wife (obviously not her) coming into my life a dozen or so years later—everything moving beyond reach forever.

Jeez, how the hell did she get herself pregnant?

# VIP Escort

*Diary of a Rich Man's Girl*

### 15th *June;*

I LOOK AT THE GIRL staring back at me in the mirror, and love her. On top of my hospitality profession, I've gained cosmetology and hair-dressing skills from beauty pageants since I joined the University of Nairobi. I even entertained the idea of modelling at some point, but it was a bad, misinformed career move after a series of débâcles on the runway and virulent censures by the judges. But I had a good hand with brush, eyeliner, and mascara.

I hear the soles of this week's client's shoes on the slate floor of the Nyali Beach Hotel presidential suite. He had gone to the beach to banquet his lusty eyes on other women's busts, butts, and thighs. I refused to accompany him even if he had paid me to escort him wherever he went for the weekend. His being away was the only chance I had to get his credit and debit cards details, feed them into my laptop (a birthday present by some blue chip company director who had tried all his best to impress me) then activate the software that would siphon his money and credit it to my Bank of Scotland account in a matter of minutes.

I have to play what he paid me to. Still, of all clients I've had, I don't like him in the least: he snores like a locomotive machine and farts in his sleep, his voice is like a bray, he says 'Gosh!' like a woman, he stares at other women's cleavages and exposed body parts and ogles at them in their bikinis, he talks to all women as though he has slept with them, and, even if he tries, he's not an appreciative lover. Heck, he ain't good in bed as he thinks he is. He pretends to be concerned about me, but all he's concerned about is the worth he's getting for his money from my body.

Fred's his name. He's a 55-year-old geezer with a hard belly, his hair at the late thinning stage on the pate of his big head, and he spends his time brokering connections for political enthusiasts. He thinks he's important, but he's nothing.

He enters and smiles at me. Well, I do what he paid me, and what I get paid, to do. I step into his embrace and kiss him slowly, languorously. He pushes me towards the bed, and I know what to do.

I lie there like a Czar, close my eyes, and endure.

# Love & Life

# Diary of a Bachelor

*Friday 13ᵗʰ April*

I CAME TO THE VERDICT that I loved her when, after so many nights of endless passion till the break of the day, she seemed not to get enough. It even crossed my mind that I could marry her (seriously?) and spend the rest of my terribly miserable life with her.

The whole thing had an air of a club Kafkaesqueness where you take the bartender who gets prettier and prettier with every bottle she serves you, only for her to go and remove her dentures before the shenanigans. You wake up the following day with self-hate weighing down on you like a millstone.

Realising that I had said some things in a

passionate haze and would probably regret them hit me like a tornado. Did I just tell her that I wanted us to have a baby? No, definitely not. What I had actually said was, "I want to have you, babe."

Turns out that anything I said because her ballooning boobs were smiling at me was circumstantial and can't be used against me in court(ship).

Marriage, for me, is an undertaking that implies some faith in a theoretical future, a projection of paired lines running forward through time, growing apart and separate from one another until they become totally different masquerades of what they once were. It is a doctrine I cannot entirely credit, nor am I sure it would be a welcomed proposition without pretence to make me feel like a better human being and supposed to share God knows what in her life when I well know that sharing has never been humanity's defining attribute.

"Babe, yesterday I was drunk with your hormones and other pheromonal stuff. It slurred my speech. Did I say something I might be sorry for? Of course not, I hope. But if I said, I am sorry, I didn't mean it," I told her when I came to my senses.

She gave me the look (that a woman would give you when you've just called her 'bitch') and said, "Seriously, Dave? Yeah, whatever," and slammed the door shut on her way out.

# Salome

I HAVE HAD MANY WOMEN in my life. I can smell the sweet perfume of one, hear the melodic singing of another, nod to the lyrical tunes of one Esther; recite Rheina's poems; dance to the tunes of Fay's music; and listen to the R&Bs Mia dedicated to me. Country music that Cindy loved plays in the background, and Melly's *Someday* by Michael Learns is a constant reminder of what used to be. I see Monica strip-dance before me, Mira teaching me what my mother never did, and I will never forget how Becky kissed.

But no one is like Salome.

Her eyes, her laughter, her playful self,

her kisses, her embrace, her lips, her body, her splendour, her magnificence, her inner beauty—no human woman can match Salome. Angel embodied.

But I hurt Salome.

I walked out on her.

I have gallivanted for years seeking unbridled pleasure in solicitous liaisons; roamed the streets picking anyone who smiled at me, scooped the flirt of the year award, cat-walked with grace no model ever mustered, or who showed too much body and booty.

It seems like a lifetime that I adored this splendid creature, like a lifetime that I had known her—Salome, my body and soul.

I must go back to Salome.

I just hope she'd be there, waiting and single.

# Single Ladies

*Diary of a Spinster*

**28<sup>th</sup> February,**

TOMORROW IS MY DAUGHTER'S WEDDING. At least she has had something in her life. Guess I have not been a model mother. I never even recognised myself as a mother, let alone scooping the Mother of the Day Award.

To the best of my ignorant knowledge, I've prepared her for the evil day. She has just left for the hen party to cleanse herself of the sins of singlehood in readiness for life imprisonment tomorrow.

My usual lullaby crooner, whiskey, is doing nothing but bring my past reeling back to me. My college days, the parties and the drinking, the guy who took the drinking and my weekends with the girls away because I was always with him drinking whatever his body secreted. The shenanigans that ended up producing Shannon and the detonation of the relationship blowing everything to smithereens, his walking out on me and severing all connection even for his daughter because I refused to abort.

Then my job as an insurance sales lady. I was a productive employee because my performance never dropped to attract the manager's attention. I used more than what they teach at sales and marketing schools. The clients were my many boyfriends who were constantly changing faces in my house, confusing Shannon, a series and a progression with the older and nicer ones coming first and the younger ones coming later when my body began to thicken and skin wrinkle. I had not wanted to be with them. Most of them were not my type or not as attractive. Miss Independence had made me feel sloth acquiescence: I was having this 'I'm-a-bachelorette' thingy and in control of my life where Shannon was my world.

I gave Shannon everything she wanted and needed but a father figure. I was her mom and dad, and when I grew up, I quit selling insurance policies and my body as a bonus, invested my life's gains in real estate and built myself a cold home. Everything stopped mattering but my lovely daughter.

The landscape behind me—the past, places, and people—is dead and long gone.

Shannon is getting married tomorrow. I've done what I could for her. She has made rules for herself, and he has agreed to abide by them. Love, such a blind thing. She thinks rules aren't broken. Marriage is just a time bomb waiting to explode.

Sixty years and a daughter who didn't see a role model in her mother is quite a feat. I've seen it all, and tomorrow shall see more—my daughter's incarceration. I hope I shall be around for her when the mansion of her delusion would be blown apart, but I don't wish it.

Now I think the whiskey has come around to doing what I intended.

Sweat dreams!

# Stolen From the Altar

*MEN DON'T CRY. GOD FORBID!*

When the Pastor said 'If there's anyone against these two becoming two in one, come out now or forever keep your peace', I did not expect anyone to.

And then he did.

No one could have *photoshopped* the real him. Not even plastic surgery would have done the trick.

Stupefied, I watched the man who had been dead for seven years walk down the aisle to the front of the church where I stood, just seconds away from officially owning the most beautiful woman in the world, the love of my life. All was morgue silent; you could have heard a pin drop and pick it.

Mouths agape, the congregation watched in debilitating flabbergast the unfolding spectacle. A cold breeze whipped sharply, stung my cheeks and watered my eyes.

All my efforts had been in vain; seven years of getting Valencia to accept that her beloved, anorexic version of a Harry Porter boyfriend was dead and gone.

I fell in love with Valencia when my brother brought her home to introduce her to the family. I couldn't allow my brother, the family Romeo, to have her. Our lifelong sibling rivalry resuscitated, and the mother of all battles ensued—*Operation Love Valencia*. Diplomacy never worked, yet I couldn't concede defeat even though Valencia loved Damian like crazy. Every *body* was against me, the family's black sheep.

Then it happened—the accident that killed Damian and almost paralysed Valencia, all my craft. What do you think? I am a medical doctor and know people with the *Gifted Hands* of Ben Carson. At least Valencia lived. Damian's body was never found because he was reduced to cinders.

And at last, Valencia was all mine.

Now, I was staring at Damian's handsome face, not even with a single scar or a single strand of hair missing. Mixed feelings crawled up to me, and I felt like crying.

Don't cry, I told myself.

Then the strangest thing happened. Instead of fainting, as it happens in Nollywood, Valencia rushed to the man we all knew was dead. They hugged and kissed—they ought to get a room, you know.

I stared defiantly at Damian, looked at the couple making out in front of the church and pitied the pathetic figure that was me.

I held back the tears.

*Men don't cry.*

It hurt to see Valencia happy with Damian, who, mysteriously, was alive.

And I could never show how much it hurt to know that Valencia was not happy with me.

# Too Busy for Life

"THAT GIRL WILL SLIP THROUGH your fingers," my mother said. "It'd be stupid of you."

"And what makes you think so?" I asked her.

"Well, you know, she's too patient with you, understands you, and cares. She's the only one who's persevered till this time despite your missing in action and disappearing acts," Mother told me. "God, she loves you."

"Absolutely," I said. "And I would like to point out that our wedding plans are underway."

"Underway? I don't like that word. That's

what you said last time, before bolting to Somalia, and the last, before disappearing to God knows where."

"Mom, don't be so condescending."

"Condescending? Me?" she seemed startled if not hurt. "I am your mother, and I need you to …"

"Marry—" I finished for her.

"Seems like you still remember."

That got my father's attention, who had been playing fence-sitter all along.

"We want to see our grandchildren before we die," he chimed in. "Look at your peers— Joseph, Peter and David—they all have grown kids."

"Yeah, and that's because I am too busy for such a life. Military ain't the career for the family I want."

"And what's that?" asked my mother.

"I don't want to be an absentee father and husband."

"Cecilia understands this, and she loves you the way you are. Can't you recognise gold when you strike one?"

"Mom, I am too busy right now," I said. "If you'll excuse me, I've got a plane to catch."

# Opium of the People

# Church Hypocritical

THE RT REV BISHOP ALFRED Rotich went straight to the Vatican after landing in Rome. It was the umpteenth time he was summoned to the Vatican in the past month.

A chauffeured limo bearing Vatican diplomatic plates glided down the Via della Conciliazione to St Peter's Basilica. It avoided the main entrance used mainly by pilgrims and tourists and veered to the right.

Ten minutes later, Bishop Rotich walked the long corridors to the papal chambers. They were vast, with floor-to-ceiling oak doors, red carpet, polished marble tiles, and sparkling chandeliers.

He knocked on the double doors, and a prelate yanked them open.

The Pope was seated behind his golden desk, seemingly in deep thought. The Pope rose from his seat to receive him, and Bishop Rotich knelt, more of a curtsy than the customary Catholic practice, and kissed the Pope's Fisherman's Ring. "Holy Father," he said.

"Bishop, thanks for coming so promptly."

Bishop Rotich got to his feet. "At your service, Holy Father."

Pope Leo XXIII gestured for Bishop Rotich to sit. "I am certain you know why you were summoned?"

The bishop said nothing but looked at the Pope.

"I think you understand what you've already caused the church—shame, disgrace, disrepute—with your 'The Truth Should be told' crusade. Well, the rock of the church has stood the test of time for over 2000 years. What makes you think you could shake that?

"You have even gone to the point of questioning the Pope's—*my*—infallibility. These secrets you purport to tell the world, have you thought of what they would do to the church, to the billions of Catholics out there?"

Bishop Rotich frowned but said nothing.

"Revelations of such magnitude to the public would do great harm and havoc to the church than meets the eye. Reverend Bishop, the past is better left buried as it has been, for with the dead is everything dark, grave and dangerous. Don't open the Pandora's Box."

"Have you no courage, Holy Father? The faith of over 2000 years can't be shaken by a startling truth. In any case, it should be strengthened."

"I get it that you are not willing to stop your lunatic rave. Despite the warnings Mother Church has given you, you've continued with your insane allegations."

Bishop Rotich felt pain like a sword pierce his heart. To the world, he was a whistle-blower; to the church, he was a heretic, apostate; but to him, he was a shrewd servant of God.

He was telling the world things kept from them by the church, secrets closely protected by the Catholic Church dating back to the time of Christ, the Vatican's amorous scandals—financial and sexual—cult worship and all. The Catholic Church was doomed, or its faith would be stronger than ever.

"With all due respect, Holy Father, I intend no harm to the church. However, don't you think of how hypocritical we are, telling people to confess their sins, reveal their dark secrets to us whence we don't confess ourselves, and are custodians of dangerous secrets?

"And all these trappings of power? Christ Himself was a poor tramp with nowhere to lay His head. But look—all this vast wealth, do you really need it, Holy Father? We live in mansions of human anguish, crowned with pomp and live in gilded rooms while the flocks we shepherd languish in poverty.

"In your life, Holy Father, have you ever stayed awake the whole night with a sick child, his fever on the highs, hoping to get a cent to buy medicine, only to be told a God who lives somewhere unreachable wants you to offer Him money or whatever so that you could be blessed? No, I guess not! The offertory we tell people to offer pays for this opulence. Do you ever think of how many people go hungry just to bring that cent because the church said God wants them to do so?"

"Bishop, Mother Church has a reputation to preserve, status and traditions to maintain."

"Don't you think it's time this charade stopped?"

"You leave me no choice, Bishop," Pope Leo said, opening a drawer of his ornate desk. He took a sealed envelope with the Papal Seal on it and handed it over to Bishop Rotich.

"I know it is not my responsibility to do this, but I have to. That's why I asked to see you personally. I hoped, against all hope, I'd change your mind. But I guess we're done here, Bishop. You are excommunicated!"

Bishop Rotich felt a jolt of electricity go through him. "Excommunicated?"

"As of now, the Roman Catholic Church does not recognize you. You know the rest."

# Dope Mother

"MY SWEET CHILDREN," MWANAISHA SAID." Work and read all the time. Do not be like me. You can't salvage me. I am a goner."

"Mama, don't say that," Mwajuma, her eldest daughter, said. "We can't watch you …"

"Mwajuma, how many times have I told you to leave me alone?" Mwanaisha's hackles were beginning to rise. It was the effect of the drug she had taken. She could no longer control herself. "Leave me alone. It is my life."

Mwanaisha was twelve when she was first introduced to drugs. They used to make her feel hyper, on top of the world. They opened a new world for her, a world she had never known existed; the world of sex and fantasy. All she could show of the shenanigans that accompanied were her three daughters whose fathers she had no idea who or where they were.

But thank God her children were not like her. Her parents had whisked them away from her when they knew of her situation. They were getting the best upbringing and education.

Since she was hustled into the Centre from the Hospital she was doing better, and her daughters were allowed to visit her. That was good. However, the best part was that she still had her constant supply of methamphetamine hydrochloride, meth in the streets, and the new drug in town.

"Are you happy living here? This way …?"

The expression that crossed Mwanaisha's face swallowed the words her daughter was about to say.

Visit time was over!

# End of Time Sermon

The self-styled, self-proclaimed prophet-of-doom-turned-street-preacher—formerly the Prefect of the Congregation of Faith in the Vatican—walked down the streets of Nairobi in a gallop. His custom-tailored *Armani* suit—his idea of sackcloth—made him stand out in the unprecedented throng of busy Nairobians.

Clutched in his armpit was a leather-bound bible, the only arsenal in his war on the Ancient Serpent. As he crossed beneath the concrete arch into *Uhuru Gardens,* he scanned the crowds as though he might find a familiar face: a brat was yelling at his mother he wanted PS2 Six; a couple showering their little bundle of joy with so much love than it was necessary; lovebirds canoodling under the palm-thatched shades; college womanisers teasing coquettish, scantily dressed *houris*; lusty couples kissing in the open, doing what they are supposed to do in their dark, tart-jaded privacies in public; a lone dude with a paperback—people locked in their own strange worlds. They all seemed absorbed. Taken in; too busy for the world around them.

This is where it would start. And end. Probably. Preach the sermon of doom, fight the ancient prostitute of Babylon. Wake people from their apathy, he said to himself.

He very well knew that people of this age know way too much. He knew Matthew twenty-four verse five by heart. *Many men, claiming to speak for me, will come and say, 'I am the Messiah!' and they will deceive many people.* People do not listen to preachers because of that single verse.

He opened his bible and read from his heart the book of Revelation. He tried to raise his voice—not even a single soul of the doomed race seemed roused. He moved around, preaching. Many thought he was crazy, one of the lunatic preachers who have crept into the church today.

People were engrossed in their own worlds. Many young, damned souls had their ears muffed by iPod buds; others were over-fondling. Hawkers were selling their merchandise like nothing was going on.

Just about time, he thought and raised his voice above the clatter and disorganised hum of the park.

When his throat was almost drying up, and his voice became a deep, hoarse whisper, he decided to take a break. During the five-minute break, his life in another world hurtled back on him.

He served 30 years, not counting the 12 he was in different seminaries studying the hidden truths of Mother Church, in the Catholic Church faithfully, only to be excommunicated for knowing what he ought not to have known and challenging Papal infallibility.

Being the Prefect of the Congregation of Faith was an achievement, and getting his way into the conclave was another, but not being anyone's pawn was a slammer. All he had to do was maintain his aim—fight the Ancient Serpent to the very end.

When he stood up again, he was all pumped up.

"The time has come to destroy those who destroy the earth," the renegade preacher continued.

# Gospels of Damnation

"WHAT'S WRONG WITH THE WORLD today?" Pastor Winfred asked her congregation. "How do you expect our children to be morally upright when what we do is preach the gospels of damnation to them?" Her voice rose above the din of everything else, amplified a thousand times by the loudspeakers piercing the streets from Central Park.

"TVs today are over-pumped with concoctions of estrogen and testosterone, too much sex being advocated for by *Safe Sex and Contraceptives Campaigns*. There are too many adverts for hedonism, crime, violence, perversion, injustice, and vengeance.

"Gone are the sermons of abstinence, respect for human dignity and life, parental guidance and G-Rating what's broadcasted on TV. Communication has been confined to gadgets of vanity and profanity, parenting left to Mr & Mrs Google and a young unmarried couple you call Facebook and Twitter in search of money that's never enough. Not to mention that the Bible, the Qur'an, and other religious texts are now an application on your iPhones and BlackBerries.

"When I look at humanity today, I feel sorry for being alive. We live the gospels of damnation to the dire neglect of the true gospels of salvation." Pastor Winfred scanned the masses before continuing.

All was silent; you could have thought Central Park was a morgue.

# Street Mother

"I WANT TO GO BACK to the streets," Grace Njeri said. "This is not where we should be."

"Mother, you can't say that," replied Shiko, Grace's 10-year-old daughter. "We have just been given another chance in life."

Her daughter was lecturing her again, Grace realised. Her wiser-than-her-years daughter. Ten but going 20. She really wished she could be a good mother.

Grace missed the streets—sniffing coke, taking brown sugar, smoking pot, and living a carefree life.

"I don't like this home. We should go back to where we came from. We were free out there. No one told us when to sleep and wake up, to wash clothes, or what to do."

"But Mom, they said they would take us to school, pay the fees and give us jobs. I want to go to school, Mommy."

"School?" Grace smiled with genuine amusement. *"Hii serikali ya Kibaki ni bure kabisa.* Do you think this useless Kibaki government will do that? People like us don't go to school. We are outcasts, cursed. For how long do I have to tell you that?"

"But that's what they told us when they brought us to this home."

"Shiko, my dear. Don't you know that they just wanted to clean their streets? We are a menace."

Shiko, the smart street kid, stared at her mother in bewilderment. Though she used to sneak to go to school, her mother always told her that she was not like other kids. She smoked pot and sniffed glue; coke, crack, and acid was her ice cream and candies. That's why she was different.

*"Mi nataka kwenda shulee ..."*

Grace felt like smothering her daughter.

"Kibaki brought free primary education,"

Grace told her daughter. "Go to school if you want, *lakini usiniitishe kitu.*"

# The Minister's Daughter

BECKY WAS ON HER FIFTH Smirnoff Black Ice. *Panty Remover*. That's what they called it. Take two, and you want to drop your pants for anything that qualifies as male or would make that waltzing in your pants go away.

"Ain't that guy cute?" Becky asked her cousin, Linnet, in a drunken stupor.

"Becky, you need to slow down," Linnet said, "seriously."

"Leave me alone, bitch."

Linnet said nothing. She knew that the alcohol was beginning to take a toll on Becky. She had better do something before it was late.

A loud shriek of laughter pierced the din

in the club, drawing blank stares from every table, even from the dance floor.

It was Becky. She was taking it to the floor, bottle in one hand, glass in the other.

Seriously, she needed to slow down.

Linnet always took care of Becky.

Halfway to where Becky was, Linnet saw Becky wobble, stagger, and start going down.

A wave of nausea swept through Becky like a tsunami. She felt everything that had been churning in her stomach jump up to the throat as dizziness invaded her.

In slow motion, Becky felt all her bones melt away, and she started going down. She groped for an invisible wall to lever herself, only to find nothing. As if it was on cue, the contents in her stomach forced their way through her small mouth.

"I've got her," a male voice said as strong arms caught her before she could hit the hard floor. She was led to a room recognised by the pungent smell.

"Don't mind us, ladies," the voice said. "We're fine."

She was bent over at the toilet bowl, where she emptied all the contents of her stomach.

God, she hated herself for letting her cousin down.

Of all people, it was Linnet who didn't preach to her. Her father, pastor and a self-proclaimed prophet of doom was the strictest father in the world. Her mother came in second with her Draconian rules and primitive disciplinary mechanisms.

Becky was now regaining consciousness, and the nice guy attending to her was wiping her face with a soft piece of cloth after splashing cold water on her.

"You shouldn't be drinking that stuff if you're not used to it, you know."

*Go to hell ... what?*

She had heard that voice a million and one times.

"Dad!" Becky said before fading out of consciousness.

# Conspiracies & Conspirators

# Terrorist's Creed

DEBRA SHIKANDA, POPULARLY KNOWN AS Lady DeeBee (DB), rolled the beads of her rosary, her baptism gift by her mother, her gaze fixed on the wooden crucifix above the altar. She had just finished reciting the joyful and sorrowful mysteries. She was now starting the light mysteries.

*Hail Mary full of grace* ... She repeated for the umpteenth time. *Pray for us sinners, now and the hour of our death. Amen.*

So much lay ahead of her: her mission, her legacy to the world. She could smell her looming death there in the church, but she was ready. Not afraid to die. She was dying for a purpose, a holy death.

Everything had been taken care of—the money would be wired to her mother's account once the mission was accomplished.

*Forgive me, Father, for I have sinned,* she prayed. *Forgive me, mother. I am so sorry I had to do this.*

*Glory be to the Father, and to the Son, and to the Holy Spirit, as it was in the beginning, is now, forever and ever. Amen.*

At exactly 1415Hrs GMT+3, Debra walked into the US Embassy building in Nairobi, Kenya. She went through the top-notch security checks and was cleared. Phase one was over.

Once inside, she went straight to her contact. Being one of the most celebrated up-and-coming musicians in the country, she was to perform her debut hit single—*For the Love of the World*—during the handing-over ceremony between the outgoing and incoming US Ambassador to Kenya. High-ranking US government officials were in attendance, including the Secretary of State.

"*Salaam Alaikum,* Khadija," her contact said when he saw her.

"What's the count?" She asked instead.

"Seven hundred. Five hundred Americans."

"Quite a number."

"You can do this. Just be calm."

"I've made my choice. My decision. There's no turning back." God had not saved them all. She would do it. It was about time.

*"Wa Alaikum Salaam,* Abdul," Lady DeeBee said as she turned to go.

When her time to perform came, she walked up the stage, amid cheers and sophisticated ululations, to do her thing, perform her *For the Love of the World* single that had brought her to the international spotlight from Nairobi. It was selling more in America than at home.

*God, I don't want to see their faces. I won't look at them,* she said to herself.

All eyes were on her as she took the mic and made the first moves that had become her trademark before stopping and saying something that startled everyone before all hell broke loose.

"I am doing this for the glory of Islam and Allah."

As she adjusted the microphone in her hand, she flipped on the discreetly concealed switch and, at the same time, the one on her bra.

The forty-storey building shook right from the foundation, explosions going off simultaneously from different locations.

# The 13<sup>th</sup> President of Kenya

*Nairobi, Kenya,*
*Friday 13<sup>th</sup> December 2097;*
*9:30 a.m.;*

IN 2011, NUCLEAR ENERGY WAS discovered in Kenya. Sooner than later, nuclear plants were built all over the country.

Sixty years later, one of the reactors in Nairobi exploded. The radiation it spewed was 10 times Hiroshima's. Over a million people died from the exposure. Another seven million were exposed to date. The result was a trail of cancers and genetic abnormalities.

Now, another wave of the tragedy was

beginning. Kenya Medical Research Institute (KEMRI) reported a 45 per cent increase in birth defects.

The president had decided on a permanent solution—to shut down all the plants.

President Olivia Chivala Munyi-Lee left her impromptu cabinet meeting in the middle. The UN was calling. Despite refusing to take the calls, the White House persisted.

*Now what?*

She knew what the White House, headquarters of the United Nations, wanted—to threaten her again with sanctions and God knows what else if she did not change her stand on shutting down all the nuclear plants in the country. Hell, come what may, she was going to. It was her country, her turf.

An hour later, her motorcade glided along Mombasa Road to the plant's site that had exploded 25 years before. It was the 26th Memorial of the tragedy, just after commemorating the 134th *Jamhuri* Day.

"Twenty-six years today, we're gathered here to commemorate the tragedy that robbed us of our beloved, men and women who suffered most from the mistakes of our actions.

Others gave up their lives and future to save this country—firemen, Red Cross workers, volunteers, disaster managers, our gallant Kenya Defence Forces personnel and those who came to build the first shield to entomb the reactor.

"We lost those dear and close to us in that tragic accident, but the pains it caused will live with us for generations to come. Genealogies were forever altered—inoperable tumours, mental retardation, genetic configurations, and other effects of the radiation.

"Let us put an end to this. Let's all say 'never again'. Let's all unite and say NO to the West who've been threatening us with sanctions and all if we take this bold step.

"Today, a new steel dome will seal this reactor for good. The sarcophagus will be forever a memorial for the lives lost 26 years ago, and all other nuclear plants all over the country will be shut down."

The crowd cheered and clapped, and reporters scrambled for space as their camera flashes blinded the 13th President, CGH, and Commander-in-Chief of the Defence Forces of the Republic of Kenya.

Olivia paused as though for effect, scanning the crowds. It was just about time she dropped the bombshell—she was running for another term (against the constitution).

From the corners of her eyes, she glimpsed someone she knew, her principal advisor and husband, and smiled at him; a fraction of a nanosecond before she knew a 12.7mm bullet had hit her from seven kilometres at the speed of light, spattering her brains all over.

# The 66th POTUS

"BARACK OBAMA CAMPAIGNED ON A plat-form of change," Michelle Obama III said, her voice amplified a million times by the speakers. "And here I am campaigning on the same platform, though a Republican."

There were cheers and ululations from her Republican supporters. From mayor to governor to senator, she had served her people well. She thought it was time for her to go for the top job.

"You wonder what change I am promising. Unlike all what politicians do, I am not going to dangle my bait for you to jump for. I will bring great change to this country once I am elected. My 'Yes We Can' slogan ain't that of my ancestor, Barack Obama, the 44th President of the United States (POTUS).

"The question is, would you trust me to bring change after or before you elect me? And please don't say 'In God We Trust'. I am asking you to trust me."

This was the last campaign rally the Republican Party held before the elections. Michelle Obama III, a Nigerian-born American, was confident she would be the first African female president of the USA.

She won unprecedentedly, with over a million votes on her Democrat rival, a descendant of George Washington.

On the same day as when Barack Obama was inaugurated, she became the 66th President of the United States of America. Then, she made her first speech.

"We are, and we'll always be, the United States of America," she began her speech with words once used by Barack Obama. After thanking the people of America for electing her the president, she told the whole world what her 'Yes We Can' change platform was about.

"I must say that when I was the mayor of San Francisco, then governor and senator all through, I vowed to be a wind of change if, and when, I became the president. I am afraid that some quarters may feel that I am treading on dangerous grounds, maybe wish you had not elected me as your president."

Now, that caught everybody off guard. All the ululations died, and a thick blanket of silence descended upon the crowds, all waiting to hear what the president had to say.

"Today, as we celebrate this great and monumental step in the history of America, I am certain many among you may see what I am about to say as a threat, but I assure you it would not be so.

"It is something that I convinced myself that it'd be courageous to see a world more peaceful, healthier, and in bountiful harvests; kind of paradise on earth.

"My vow was this: my leadership would be of absolute honesty, integrity, and more in touch with those I lead; create a home for everyone full of peace and love, happiness and freedom. Security is for all, not a few, for this country belongs to us, both the leaders and the led."

A wave of disbelief spread through the astonished crowds worldwide, where people were glued to TV sets.

"If I lead the people who elected me, why should I be afraid of them, be surrounded by dozens of armed men and women to protect me? If only we could see the world through the eyes of a child, we would hold the earth in our arms.

"From now onwards, there'd be no Secret Service to protect me. The National Security Agency would not spy on any other country. The United States of America would not impose any policy on other countries. America would down all her nuclear, biological and chemical weapons, all WMDs would be destroyed, US Army troops worldwide would withdraw ASAP, and the USA would be a home to everyone. Peace, love and harmony need no NBCs, WMDs, and violence.

"We claim to be leaders of the people, but what do we do? We are surrounded by accumulated wealth and vast riches, protected from those whom we call our fellow countrymen and brethren by elite commandos on taxpayers' dime while all over the world are naked, sick and hungry men, women, and children."

Everybody was silent; you could have thought the whole world was in a post-Armageddon trance.

"The White House is not my residence. My home, where Mrs Smith and Tommy are neighbours, is … I am appealing to all world leaders to see it this way, a home we can live happily, carefree, free and safe.

"This is my change, and 'Yes, We Can!'"

# The Blood of Our People

"THE DEPOSIT HAS ALREADY BEEN credited," Faisal al Nasi listened. "You can go on with the plan. Your family will be well taken care of if you die from this."

"*Allahu Akhubar*," Faisal said to the caller.

"*Assalaam Aleikum*, Faisal."

"*Wa Aleikum salaam*," he said as the caller hung up.

Faisal checked his luggage again. It was a camera, specially made to accommodate his customised Berretta pistol and a press pass. He was the phantom representative of the phantom *Independent News* newspaper at the prime minister's conference in the afternoon.

At exactly two o'clock, the prime minister, campaigning for the presidency, entered the Hilton Hotel's Tsavo Ballroom right on schedule.

He walked to the bouquet of microphones at the podium, leaned toward the microphones, and his voice boomed out over the expectant silence.

"Every day I see this country try to rise on shaky legs—burdened by debt and poverty, death and violence, rife with graft and corruption—I convince myself that we need a leader.

"Today, we pay for the sins of our fathers—stealing from public coffers, political assassinations, tribal clashes and masterminded post-election chaos, graft (Anglo-leasing, Goldenberg, Grand Regency) and other scandals.

"My family has been connected to such crimes, I don't deny or confirm it, but I am on this alone. I can't be guilty of my family's sins and crimes. That is why I insist I am the man this country needs.

"It is time for a new era. Brothers and sisters, we've suffered enough from our past sins. Enough is enough. The blood of our people that has been shed so far is sacrifice enough."

The Prime Minister let his pain ring out. He knew how it looked on camera—the determined face of reform and liberation for the third republic.

"The blood of our people—men, women and children, victims of post-poll chaos, political figures who were assassinated, and police officers who die in the course of their duty trying to maintain law and order in a seemingly lawless society. We may forget them, but not their sacrifice."

Reporters clung to their cameras and notebooks as though their lives depended on them. There were other presidential candidates, but only the Prime Minister had the country by the spell. They ridiculed and lambasted him in the press, but he knew he was the president the country needed.

"While we put an end to one chapter of our history, let's do it once and for all. Blood is the tincture of true sacrifice, and that's what our people have done. So, let's not let their sacrifices go unyielded."

At the forest of the press, Faisal knew that his time had come. He was not to waste it. He reached for his concealed gun, retrieved it and pointed it at the prime minister.

Faisal fired. Twice. The prime minister went down a moment before he fired again.

Faisal never knew whether his mission was accomplished.

That evening, the news was abuzz with the failed assassination attempt. As the prime minister watched the news at his official residence, his mind went back to the fateful afternoon.

His bodyguards had pulled him down behind the podium, right on cue, as cries erupted from the crowd. Pandemonium had ruled for a breath.

It had gone well. Just as planned.

The shooter had been shot by the premier's security detail. Died instantly. It had not been difficult to convince Faisal that he was doing it for the glory of Islam and Allah.

After all, his was among 'the blood of our people' shed for the country's liberation.

# The Criminal Lawyer

"THIS ISN'T PERSONAL, IS IT, Mr Mungai?" asked Marwa as they walked along the long corridor to Judge Adan Mohammed's chambers. The judge had called for a recess and summoned the two lawyers to his chambers to deliberate on the sentence.

"No," replied Mungai, the prosecutor. "Not in the slightest. One thing that has made me come this far in my career is that I detached emotions, grudges and beef from my prosecution equation and remained with truth and justice as the common denominator. We may have crossed paths with your client's father, punches and blows thrown—figuratively—but your client is not on my shit list. He is on my criminal list. I wouldn't want to rid society of your client on a vendetta. With the spate of murders he has committed, robberies he has orchestrated and arsenal found in his house—as though he was preparing for a war—it's automatic that the court gives him the noose, sheer luck if it's life. And don't tell me you don't know this, counsel?"

Marwa smiled, and, suddenly, his face did not seem as sharp as it was in court a moment ago defending a bank robber, murderer, and rapist.

"I do," Marwa said. "And don't tell me you don't know when a lawyer is performing for the cameras too … even if the media weren't there. You know how it is with clients. They like to see some drama for their money. That's the babe of criminal lawyers."

His smile stayed on the prosecutor until they entered Judge Adan's chambers.

"You almost went for each other's throats in there," Judge Adan said when the two attorneys-at-law were seated opposite him. "Needn't I tell you how to behave in a courtroom? You know that school-kids drama in my court is a no-no." The judge paused. "However, you know why I called you here."

The two lawyers sat silently for a moment, wondering who would be the first to say something.

"Prosecution calls for a death sentence, and not because we want to make an example because of who he is …"

"My client is guilty," Marwa said, "but that does not mean frying him for all hell takes. I've talked with his father. Senator Mutuma Nzilo does not want to see his son go away forever or anything like that, but a short spell in jail might bring back his senses. If he has any left."

"Are you suggesting a lesser punishment or sentence …?"

"No, no. Not in the least. I have discussed this with Senator Mutuma, and he wants his criminal son, who's an embarrassment to him and the family, to have a taste of the rule of law."

"I hear what you are saying, counsellor," Judge Adan said, "but with the magnitude of your client's crime life, imprisonment is a sentence too lenient."

"I understand that," Marwa said. "Senator Mutuma has already talked with the Attorney General and the President. My client would be granted a presidential pardon after three years, off the record, of course. Senator Mutuma has played a significant role in the just concluded elections. President Mambo owes him a few too."

"If that's the case," the prosecutor said, "prosecution rests its case."

"Good, you just made this stalemate easier. Counsel here has evidence enough to exonerate his client of the criminal charges, so is prosecution to put the accused on death row. Off the record, you should drop by for dinner sometimes, gentlemen," the judge said.

# The Crying President

*October 10, 8:30 p.m.;*
*Nairobi, Kenya.*

FLORENCE GACHANJA-WILLIAMS WAITED FOR the cameras to be set up. She had already been prepped, her make-up done and rehearsed her speech. The media was already waiting to popularise her, the newest presidential candidate to join the race to State House.

But she was no ordinary politician—she was young, just turned 23, and with brains to match her age. Her intellect told her that she could go for it; she was the president that the country needed.

Age was just numbers!

However, she was ready to face the seasoned, veteran politicians of Kenyan politics, some of whom were an enigma.

When given the thumbs up, she walked to the podium, smiled and waved at the people who had turned up for the launch of her political party, her vehicle to State House, and her manifesto.

She faced the cameras, leaned toward the microphones and began her speech, accentuating each word spat by the autocue with an Anglophone twang. She had been born and raised in Britain, but it was time she traced her roots, and with purpose.

As she spelt out her political objectives, she occasionally caught glimpses of familiar faces—ambassadors, dignitaries, and political heavyweights—faces that were the engine and fuel for her political dream.

Her speech was moving—it highlighted the burdens of debt, diseases, corruption, violence and domestic terrorism, and the scourge of tribal clashes that had become Brand Kenya in Africa and the world.

She turned to the cameras and pressed the

back of her wrists to one eye. She had used the methylated chapstick that her personal assistant (and campaign secretary) had placed on the podium to dab the edges of her wristwatch and pantsuit coat with menthol. The sting drew the required tears.

She wiped her cheek and hardened her countenance. Tears were just fine, but she did not want to appear weak.

Well, they served the purpose.

By morning the following day, all major dailies and papers that were struggling to remain in business, even the gutter press, ran her teary, beautiful face on the front page with the headline: 'The Crying President'.

# United States of Africa

*African Union Summit,*
*Abuja, Nigeria; 2066.*

"OVER A HUNDRED YEARS AGO, mid-twentieth century, African states, in a frail attempt to stand on their shaky legs, began to fight for independence from the colonialists," AU Head, a retired Kenya Defence Forces General, began his speech. "Tribal armies were formed, communities forged alliances, and warriors marched against the sophisticated colonial troops. Battles were fought, blood was shed, and lives were lost.

"Our leaders, the freedom fighters, were

branded criminals and tagged terrorists and were hunted down like game and killed if not incarcerated. They never gave up until, one by one, the invaders gave in. We celebrated what we called independence, as long as it lasted, for hardly had we started to govern ourselves when we realised that the whole independence thing was a ruse—it was granted to us. The former colonial masters controlled everything we did behind the scenes, neo-colonialism.

"We did nothing as we watched our beautiful home being plundered, looted, and our mothers being raped before our very eyes because, if we raised an eyebrow, all foreign aid would be cut; our already frail economies, burdened by debt, graft and corruption, ethnicity and Western erosion. Some of our leaders stood firm and sent away the marauding invaders; others said NO to Western interference, only for the International Community to come down upon them like a ton of a thousand bricks with sanctions and what-have-you. Not to mention how our moral and cultural fabric has been disintegrated to nihility by activists from American and European backyards, and as if that's not enough, burned to smithereens.

"Colonel Muammar Gaddafi saw a one Africa, a continent of united states. What happened? The International Community bombed the country he had built from scratch and buried him under the ruins of the cities he had once gloried.

"China has come knocking on our doors dangling the bait of infrastructural development before us. Our greed led us to jump ship, only to have murderous convicts who have no pathos for whatever they do dumped in our homes in the guise of construction supervisors. These jailbirds have killed our people with impunity, and our presidents, the fathers of our nations, play criminal lawyers for them.

"Does this mean that Africa cannot stand on her own? Must we always be funded by foreigners? Must our governments always be partners with these conspiratorial foxes? We offer their governments plausible deniability for their criminal activities—secretly financed torture camps in our precious homes, nuclear plants in our front yards; test grounds for their nuclear, biological and chemical weapons in our backyards; experimentation on human beings; and dumping ground for convicted murderers and all criminals.

"Lines of acceptable conduct have become blurred. 'Not on our soil' is the foreigners' Credo.

"Mama Africa is beautiful, rich and healthy, but has been robbed of all these before her very eyes. Nonetheless, it's not too late. We can salvage our beloved Africa from these marauding acts of our subtle enemies."

All eyes of the 54 heads of state were fixed on him. He had them under his spell. He hoped to gods and ancestors they were listening to him. What he was telling them had consequences but was necessary.

"Africa needs to be liberated. The second liberation of our beautiful home is now, this time not as a state but as One Africa. The mistakes of our past should not be repeated, our leaders being sacrificed to Western gods at NATO shrines not anymore.

"Shut all the doors that open up for foreign aid. Let's start a new Africa.

"A new Renaissance, a new homeland,

together as one.
"United States of Africa."

# Acknowledgements

I am grateful to Sadik Ali Ibrahim for the help he accorded me while writing some of the stories in this book; Victor Wekesa for being a virulent critic and editor of some of the stories; and everybody else who read and commented on my website, fans who waited for the publication of the next story eagerly and took their time to read.

And you, my reader, who has purchased this book and read it to the very end. I care about you more than you think.

# About the Author

VINCENT DE PAUL is an award-winning author, freelance writer, ardent blogger, an avant-garde poet. He has perfected and taken the flash fiction genre to a new level.

He is the author of the award-winning collection of poetry, *First Words,* and the most sensational love poetry loved the world over, *Holy Emotions* and *Holy Crimes.* His other poetry collections are *Flights of Poetic Fancy* and *Black Communion,* an anthology of New Age African poets published in Nigeria.

# DON'T MISS OUT ON MORE OF FLASH FICTION STORIES

Life on the fast lane; sex, money and crime—the holy trinity of life. Terrorists and their virgins; love, romance and marriage chastised.

**HAVE A SNEAK PREVIEW**

# Bomb Nairobi

FARIHA ABDIWEY BOARDED THE NO.9 *matatu* from Eastleigh for the last time. She had bid her family goodbye for the glory of Allah.

Once in town, Fariha went straight to her hotel room at the Hilton, Nairobi. At least she was going to die in luxury.

The room overlooked the busy Moi Avenue. She sat on the bed with the laptop that had been her toy for the past three years. She opened the heavily encrypted application on the desktop. She typed in several codes then the window popped up with the city map and the blueprints of the buildings she wanted.

Outside, the city was a buzz, the trademark

Nairobi jam; hawkers selling their wares like nothing was going on. While the application loaded, Fariha went to the window to have a final look at the city she had lived in, and had called home, all her life.

It was electrifying for Fariha to be the chosen one. She had been entrusted with the mission. "Bomb Nairobi," she had been told.

The targets had been carefully selected and unique. Kenyans will forever talk about it. The 1998 Nairobi bomb blast, the 2002 Paradise Hotel bombing in Mombasa, and the 2013 Westgate Mall siege were nothing. The real terror attack was coming. There was no such thing as too much punishment for Kenya. Kenya had interfered way too much with her people, even after being warned.

The application on her laptop opened, and the screen displayed a kaleidoscope of the city's ultra-modern buildings. Seven of those were to be annihilated.

All the targets blinked green at her. An MS-DOS command prompt window was open at the bottom of the screen showing only two words against the black background: EXECUTE, y/n?

Fariha had no doubt. It was 'y'. That's the key she hit on the laptop keyboard.

Nothing happened for some soul-annihilating seconds. Then a loud explosion from the direction of Harambee House roared like thunder. She felt the walls of her hotel room vibrate, then shake, shortly before a series of explosions rocked the city.

She rushed to the window for the last time before the hotel she was in exploded. It was Armageddon outside. The sight filled her with indescribable pride.

At last, they had taken the war to Nairobi, as they had promised. Kenya had invaded her country and killed her people. Fariha felt her blood begin to boil in accomplishment.

*"Istaqfurulah,"* she prayed.

For a little while, Fariha felt more at peace than she had ever known shortly before the Hotel Hilton tumbled down like an avalanche.

*Alhamdulilah* was her last word.

# Heroes of Somalia

*April 2012, 0730Hrs*
*DOD Headquarters,*
*Ulinzi House, Nairobi*

"WHY ARE WE LOSING SOLDIERS all of a sudden? Are you not giving them timely intelligence?" the Chief of Defence Forces asked.

"We are, sir," said the Director of Military Intelligence.

"Then what is happening? Why are they getting killed?"

"Sir, we can't control what they do at the battlefront. We do our job; leave the rest to them …."

"How many were killed in last night's attack —five, seven? Something is wrong somewhere. Our soldiers are well trained. I don't expect this growing number of casualties unless they are not well briefed before an operation."

The DMI weighed what he was about to say next. Then, "Sir, those soldiers were not killed by enemy fire …"

"What?"

*

***President's Speech,
Mashujaa Day, 2012***

"… and in addition, I applaud our gallant soldiers in Somalia for their good work so far. They have made a great sacrifice in fighting for this country. They are our heroes.

"In particular, I would like to recognise the fallen soldiers who died from the enemy's bullet. The ground that sipped their blood may dry, and their memories may fade, but their sacrifice will never be forgotten. The nation will never forget. We honour them for their valiance with the heroes' medal of the Order of Grand Warriors of Kenya ...."

*

*May 2014,*
*The Sarova Stanley Hotel, Nairobi*

"Lynn, I heard you have an investigative piece coming next week," he said over dessert. "Good work."

"Who told you?"

"I have my sources ...."

"That's not why you asked me out, is it?"

"Well—"

"You son-of-a-bitch."

"Lynn, it's national security."

"People died for this country, gave their lives. Wives were widowed, children were orphaned, and mothers were left childless. Sorrow weighs upon them. They are grieving. Come on, Peter. It's two years now, and families of some of those soldiers who died in Somalia have not been compensated, and in particular the ...."

"Lynn, you can't air that exposé. I know

you love what you do, and God knows *we* love it too, but this one can't …."

"This date is over …."

"No, it isn't," he said.

Lynn started to get up. "Sit down, Lynn!"

Against her alpha female judgement, the *Ukweli TV (UTV)* investigative reporter perched her tight, denim-clad butt on the seat she had barely vacated.

An ominous blanket of silence enveloped them before Peter tore it asunder.

"Lynn, you can't air that piece because those soldiers were not killed by enemy fire. They were traitors, Lynn."

Lynn's jaw dropped on the table and bounced twice before it dropped to the floor. Peter was still talking.

"… we had been following them for long. They were working for al-Shabaab. They always reported our troops' movement. Have you never wondered why most KDF soldiers were killed in ambushes? You are the investigative reporter …."

Lynn said nothing, just listened.

"The army can't pay them, *yet*. But they are heroes. Their families can never know the truth, Lynn. The soldiers were traitors, not heroes."

When Major Peter Thome was done, Lynn didn't say anything. Or she just decided not to.

An eternity stretched before the investigative reporter said, "I will call my producer." And with that, she rose to go.

# Mujahideen

LEILAH FARDOSA ABDIKARIM MOHAMMED disembarked the UAE Airliner at Moi International Airport, Mombasa, straight from Kismayo, and breathed in the smell of the ocean. Ever since Somalia stabilised 30 years ago, travelling had become much easier. Flights were no longer being diverted to Wajir International Airport for clearance.

It had been one hell of a journey. A near soul annihilating delay at Kismayo International Airport had gotten the better of her, but thank goodness she had now reached her destination.

Despite the coastal weather, she was in a

*burqa,* her eyes scanning the international arrivals behind the slit opening of the pall-black dress. It was much easier to dress this way in Kenya without raising suspicion than in the ever-so-paranoid West.

However, she had been warned that all airports in Kenya swarmed with armed security guards, customs, anti-terror police, security agents, and a whole horde of behavioural detection officers ever since spates of terror attacks rocked the country 50 years before.

Hyperventilating could get you picked for questioning. So was rapid eye movement. Or sweaty palms. But she knew that MIA was the easiest to slip through.

Everything was going on like a dream—albeit in a crawl—passport control, luggage screening. Then, she was out. She had made it.

Leilah took the way to her next destination imprinted on her mind. Photographic memory. That's why The Council liked her and always picked her. She never needed a map or notes.

Through grimy streets and dark alleys, which she had used only once, and at night, almost 25 years ago, she wove her way through *makuti* thatched houses and coconut plantations until she saw the ghoulish silhouette of the mosque. The slain Sheikh, who was her mentor and teacher, had given her a copy of the key to the secret door. "Just in case," he had said.

The Kenya government closed the Masjid Musa Mosque in 2014 after a series of Islamic extremism-instigated violence hit the country. Muslims were simply fighting for their freedom, demonstrating against government killings targeting them. The government spewed radicalisation propaganda.

The mosque was always being watched, but the security devils did not know that there was secret access to it.

Leilah went around the darkened mosque and found the well-concealed entrance. She fumbled for the key in her purse, extracted it and inserted it into the keyhole. When she turned it, nothing happened. But she expected it. Her identity was being verified electronically by a super-fast computer in the basement.

After what seemed like an eternity, about

twelve-and-a-half nanoseconds later, a voice asked her to say in whose arms Prophet Mohammed died.

Leilah smiled as she mouthed the secret code that The Council had given her to gain access to join her brothers and sisters.

Leilah entered the darkened mosque and was received by a portly woman in her prime.

"Welcome home, White Sister," the woman said in Arabic. "Auntie Sherafiyah awaits you."

Leilah could hear *Qiyaam al-Layl* prayer coming through the walls. The woman stopped at a tall carved door and let her inside. She didn't follow.

Auntie Sherafiyah hadn't changed a bit since Leilah last saw her. If anything, she had become glued to the wheelchair.

"Mama," Leilah said as she rushed to where Auntie Sherafiyah was anchored.

"Samantha!" Auntie Sherafiyah said.

"I've missed you so."

Leilah hugged her mother amid tears. "I'm sorry I didn't call."

Auntie Sherafiyah waved her off. "You were right not to call," she said. "This place is crawling with the infidel devils thirsting for our blood. They listen to everything. Now you are home. Sit, don't be sorry."

She was, but Leilah listened to her mother, whom everybody called Auntie Sherafiyah.

"I came without any incidence," Leilah told her mother. "Thanks to you, Mama."

"Now you are home, Samantha. Get rid of that *burqa,* and let me see my lovely daughter."

Leilah did as she was told. She tore off the stuffy dressing and stood before her mother in her European clothes, clothes from home. Her mother looked at her and grinned.

There stood the girl who, at five years old, had said without faltering that she would be Mujahideen when she grew up.

Get the latest author updates, other writing, keep informed about upcoming releases and, subscribe to email for all the latest news, get a chance to download free eBooks and win copies of his books.

Go to:

www.vdepaul.com

Blogs:

www.poeticjustnes.com
www.flashesofvices.com

**Vincent de Paul's Books**

Available for download as ebooks on

**Nuria Bookstore | Amazon Kindle | Mystery Bookstore |**

**Smashwords | Barnes & Noble | Apple iTunes**